Dear Parents:

Congratulations! Your child is taking the first steps on an exciting journey. The destination? Independent reading!

STEP INTO READING® will help your child get there. The program offers five steps to reading success. Each step includes fun stories and colorful art or photographs. In addition to original fiction and books with favorite characters, there are Step into Reading Non-Fiction Readers, Phonics Readers and Boxed Sets, Sticker Readers, and Comic Readers—a complete literacy program with something to interest every child.

Learning to Read, Step by Step!

Ready to Read   Preschool–Kindergarten
• big type and easy words • rhyme and rhythm • picture clues
For children who know the alphabet and are eager to begin reading.

Reading with Help   Preschool–Grade 1
• basic vocabulary • short sentences • simple stories
For children who recognize familiar words and sound out new words with help.

Reading on Your Own   Grades 1–3
• engaging characters • easy-to-follow plots • popular topics
For children who are ready to read on their own.

Reading Paragraphs   Grades 2–3
• challenging vocabulary • short paragraphs • exciting stories
For newly independent readers who read simple sentences with confidence.

Ready for Chapters   Grades 2–4
• chapters • longer paragraphs • full-color art
For children who want to take the plunge into chapter books but still like colorful pictures.

STEP INTO READING® is designed to give every child a successful reading experience. The grade levels are only guides; children will progress through the steps at their own speed, developing confidence in their reading.

Remember, a lifetime love of reading starts with a single step!

BARBIE and associated trademarks and trade dress are owned by, and used under license from, Mattel.
Copyright © 2020 Mattel.
www.barbie.com
Published in the United States by Random House Children's Books, a division of Penguin Random House LLC, 1745 Broadway, New York, NY 10019, and in Canada by Penguin Random House Canada Limited, Toronto.

Step into Reading, Random House, and the Random House colophon are registered trademarks of Penguin Random House LLC.

Visit us on the Web!
StepIntoReading.com
rhcbooks.com

Educators and librarians, for a variety of teaching tools, visit us at RHTeachersLibrarians.com

ISBN 978-0-593-12784-1 (trade) — ISBN 978-0-593-12785-8 (lib. bdg.)

Printed in the United States of America
10 9 8 7 6 5 4 3 2 1

Pup on the Run

adapted by Elle Stephens

based on the original screenplay by M. J. Offen

Random House 🏠 New York

Barbie loves
to help everyone.
Today she helps
Chelsea with a project.

They set

up Barbie's laptop.

Barbie puts
a pup cam
on Honey.

The camera will take
a live video
for Chelsea's class.
They can talk to Honey
through the cam, too.

Honey loves it!

Skipper and Stacie
are excited.
They are going
to a music festival.

Barbie is helping her
friend Nikki.
She is baking
cake bars.

Nikki will hand the bars out at the festival. Then people will know about Nikki's bakery.

Barbie also
helps Ken.

He has to practice
for a talent show.

They work
on his moves
by the pool.

Nikki comes to pick
up the bars.
They are in boxes.

Honey jumps up.
She jumps
into a box!

Nikki brings the boxes
to the festival.

She is ready
to hand out cake bars!

Nikki does not see
Honey pop out
of a box.

At home,
Barbie sees Honey's
pup cam on her
computer.
Honey is at the festival!

She talks to Honey
on the laptop.
"Go to Nikki!" she says.
But Honey sees
a butterfly.

Barbie goes
to look for Honey.
She does not want
to ask for help.

Barbie spots Honey!
Honey does not
see Barbie.

Honey chases
the butterfly.
Barbie chases Honey.

Stacie and Skipper
see Barbie and Honey.
They think Barbie
needs help.

Honey follows
the butterfly.
She runs
up a ladder.

Barbie follows Honey
up the ladder.
Someone takes
the ladder away!

Barbie tries
to get Honey.
She still does not want
to ask for help.

Barbie gets Honey.
But they are stuck
upside down!

Stacie, Skipper,
and Nikki find them.
Now Barbie asks
for help.

Back at home,
the girls
watch Chelsea's project.
Honey made a great video!

Barbie helped
everyone today.
They helped her,
too.

Barbie learns that
it is okay
to ask for help.
Hugs for help!